Clint Faraday
book twenty six
Curtain Death

A dense fog in the mountains that makes the carretera as much as impossible to drive. Enel Fortuna dam. Two bodies. Looks like hit-and-run. Not those two!

Clint Faraday
book twenty six
Curtain Death
(c)2012 & 2018 by C. D. Moulton

This is a work of fiction. Any resemblances to persons, living or dead, or events is purely coincidental unless otherwise stated.

Contents

About the author

CD Moulton has traveled extensively over much of the world both in the music business, where he was a rock guitarist, songwriter and arranger and in an import/export business. He has been everything from a bar owner to auto salvage (junkyard) manager, longshoreman to high steel worker, orchid grower to landscaper, tropical fish farmer to commercial fisherman. He started writing books in 1983 and has published more than 350 books as of January 1, 2023. His most popular books to date are about research with orchids, though much of his science fiction and fantasy work has proven popular. He wrote the CD Grimes, PI series, and the Det. Nick Storie series, Clint Faraday series, and many other works.

He now resides in Gualaca, Chiriqui, Panamá, where he writes books, plays music with friends, does research with orchids and medicinal plants. He has lately become involved in fighting for the rights of the indigenous people, who are among his closest friends, and in fighting the extreme corruption in the courts and police in Panamá.

He offers the free e-book, *Fading Paradise*, that explains what he has been through because of the corruption.

CD is the discoverer of the Chadam Protocol for curing cancer.

Facebook page Ambrosia peruviana for cancer.

Foggy Night

Clint stretched and reached for his coffee cup his wife, Tyna, had put there on the rail next to his hammock. The sun was just below the horizon across the Caribbean, turning the sky into a fantastic range of colors. The light breeze coming across Saigon Bay to his deck over the water gave a slightly cool hint to the daybreak.

What to do today? He had enough diving and fishing the past two days, and it had been a month since that last case, where the guy was found dead wearing a shroud. Tyna was going to be visiting family on Isla Popa and in the main comarca for a few days.

Raul Castanetas went by in his cayuca and called the Coin dega! good morning in Guayme, the Indio language. Clint waved and returned the greeting.

Maybe he'd go into the interior comarca with Tyna to visit his best friends for a couple or three days. They always welcomed him, because there was always, or so it sometimes seemed, excitement when he was around. Murders.

He drained the coffee cup and went inside to get another. He was as much as a coffee addict, and Panamanian coffee was the best to be found, particularly this. A friend grew, dried and ground it special for him and Judi Lum, his attractive nextdoor neighbor who helped him with his cases.

He was a retired PI from Florida. He had a lot more cases here than he ever had in Florida, and had proven himself to be a friend and aide to the Policía Nacionál de Panamá. He worked with Sergio Sanchez on many of his cases, there on Isla Colón, as well as in Bocas del Toro Province, generally. He worked cases all over Panamá.

He went back out to wave at Judi, watering her orchids on her deck. She wagged a finger at him in their long established ritual. He didn't wear anything before he had his morning swim and decided what to wear for whatever he planned for the day.

Judi and Clint both had large collections of orchids, as did Ben and Earl, neighbors, and any other closer friends of their nutty writer/botanist/musician friend, Dave. He went all over Panamá studying the orchids and medicinal plants.

He finished the coffee as the sun rose to seem to be sitting on the sea at the horizon. He dove into the bay, swam for about fifteen minutes, climbed back onto his deck, rinsed, and went in to put on khaki shorts and a tank top. The line from Jimmy Buffet's song went through his mind when he looked in the mirror: *Old men in tank tops, Cruising the gift shops*

Well, he wasn't that old. Sixty two.

Maybe he was. He felt good, and kept in top physical shape, so age was only a number.

He checked his computer, answered the two legitimate e-mails, erased eleven spams, and sat back.

The phone rang. He picked it up. It was a police officer from Chiriqui. Clint had worked a couple of cases with him.

"Clint? Tonio here. How are things?"

"About as perfect as it gets. You?"

"The fog's very bad here. I'm on the dam. There are two bodies a bus driver found when he was crossing as soon as the curtain thinned enough for him to see ten meters ahead. It looks like a hit-and-run, except for one small detail, as you are prone to say."

"Which is?"

"It's Miko Itumi and Jorge Sardina."

"Doesn't mean anything to me – wasn't Miko involved in that sheik thing? Isn't he in jail for the next twenty to life?"

"Got out on a technicality. Retrial starts next Tuesday."

"Technicality?"

"And Jorge Sardina was the judge, now retired, who bought a big finca just below here out of Calderas less than a week after he found the technicality."

"The judge found the technicality? Isn't that the lawyers' – of which he had four – job?"

"Why, Mr. Faraday! What are you suggesting? Judge Sardina was above reproach, except for those twelve or fifteen charges against him for corruption that the other judges threw out!"

Clint gave the phone the finger. "So? Need help?"

"I'd say yes, but you know the kind of people we'll be going after. I won't blame you for a second if you tell me to shove it up my ass!"

"Well, if you'd caught me when I had something else to do I'd probably tell you exactly that. I'll get there in about three hours. I guess you can't preserve the site that long."

"The chopper should be there about now. I knew you would want in on this one!"

"I'm giving the phone a one finger salute, with a twist!"

He heard the chopper coming into hearing and rang off to grab a few things and put on clothes that would suit the cold at 1800 meters elevation in a dense fog with a breeze.

He was aboard and on the way to the dam in six minutes. Judi waved as they rose. Tyna had kissed him goodbye so passionately he was undecided whether he should wait ... no.

This would be an interesting one – or maybe not.

<u>*Unclear View*</u>

The fog was really denser than Clint or the pilot liked as they sat on the visitor's viewpoint at the dam. The police truck was there, as were two ambulances and the big CSI van. An officer was directing the few cars, trucks, and buses that were there around the conglomeration. Tonio waved and came to the chopper to tell him what they had.

"The two were laying there as they are now when we arrived. The Changuinola bus driver, Beto Marineros, was doing the slow waltz across the dam, maybe twelve or fifteen kilometers per hour, because of the fog – it was a lot worse than now, and you can just see them now – and the glare. Doc says they were hit by a truck or bus, but he'll have to do a complete to be sure they weren't dead when they were hit.

"That'd be my guess, seeing who they were. Somebody didn't want them talking or showing anyone something.

"You can look at them. Doc says he's about through sweeping the scene.

"Now. What I've learned with the radio goes

something like: Itumi was sentenced to twenty to life, he served less than a week when the judge found what he called a large gap in the evidence. It seemed that the connection with the killings on Bocas was a knife with the victim's blood on it. The knife was now missing, somehow, and the judge, Sardina, said there had been a break in the chain of evidence security. The knife was sent to Panamá City by aeroplane. The sealed package appeared to have been opened during that flight, so it well might have become contaminated at that time.

"There was nothing to indicate the package had been opened. The judge suddenly claimed he had been informed of that fact in a sidebar, and it had slipped his mind. The police lab man who was supposed to have reported it in court now said he had told the judge the package seemed to have been torn or something, as he remembered it.

"There is no record in the trial recordings of the lab messenger ever having been in court, much less approaching the bench. The messenger now has a new job where he makes triple what he made working for the police lab.

"Duh!

"That's about it."

"What was the messenger's name?"

"It was, here it is, Santo Fernandez. Why?"

"Do you have an address?"

"At the station, yes."

"Get someone there! He might already have had his accident. Somebody's eliminating all possible witnesses.

"What about Sheik Bigmouth? What happened to him?"

"They sent him back to be prosecuted on that island he once owned. He was publicly stoned, as I understand it. Reverting back to the old law."

"Check to be sure that was done. If it was, we have a worm in this apple, right here!"

Tonio nodded and went to the radio. Doc talked with Clint for a few minutes, showing him where he thought the head had been caved in on the judge before he was run over. "They were run over by tandem wheels. They weren't hit and run over."

Clint nodded and went back to Tonio, who was getting a report.

"A man is going to Fernando's place. The sheik was definitely stoned. They refused him burial in hallowed ground or whatever. He was dumped into a pauper's grave.

"Doc's through, and the crew would prefer that I was gone, I think. They know their job. You can ride into David with me if you like."

Clint liked. He got his maleta off of the chopper

and climbed in back of the truck with the police crew. He talked with them. Two officers got off in Hornitos, and two went on into David with them.

Clint checked into the Pensión Costa Rica and cleaned up a bit. He got a call from Tonio as he was leaving. Fernandez didn't come home last night. He rather expected something on that order would be the case.

Who else would be able to testify about any of this mess? That hanger-on thug? Was he still in jail, or had he also been released on a technicality?

Clint got a good late lunch at Mi Bacata and headed for the fiscalia and the court – where he was denied access to the records.

He called Tonio, who said he was also meeting a solid wall of resistance to getting any information about the case. It seemed the reputation for corruption in that division was getting bolstered very much by this process. There were definitely more than a couple of people involved in it.

Clint remembered Dave's continuing involvement with it. Three years of fighting it, and only a slow advance against it. Politicians ran for office swearing to get rid of that corruption, then became even worse in very short time.

"They don't want this to go further. There could

only be one reason behind that!" Tonio snarled. "Well, the law reads that anyone who is involved in corruption that results in a major crime is a direct accessory. That means the ones who were involved can then be charged with accessory to murder. I intend to see they get prosecuted for that.

"Clint, I will work with you in any way I can. If we can search them out, I guarantee you they'll be prosecuted. I'm going to Panamá City with this. It's making police work useless. It has to stop."

"We can't stop it. It's too ingrained. We can slow it down some, though," Clint replied. "What was that thug's name?"

"Other than ... Lobo? I don't know. I'll look up the records. I can find that from the reports in Bocas and David and bypass those corrupt snakes in the court system."

"It will be on the police computers, so they can never be rid of it." Clint thought for a minute, then said he was going to the internet to do a little research. Maybe there was a way to find part of what they needed to know.

He went to an internet service company and sat at a machine for more than six hours, then went to dinner, then returned to the internet. A lot of things are public record. First, find a reference in the newspapers, then use a search to expand that.

It was a slow process, but he had some success.

He went to the Costa Rica and slept his seven hours, then went to the police station. Tonio was pouring over written reports. He said it was all supposed to be in the comps, but they somehow forgot to input the information.

Clint soon noticed a woman who was spending far too much time right outside of the office door. He picked up a paper and read a bit then turned as if to go to the door. She quickly went to a nearby desk and sat there to look busy. Clint had exceptional peripheral vision, so was able to never be seeming to look her way. As soon as she was away he asked Tonio about her. He hadn't noticed. He'd go along with Clint to see what she was up to.

They stayed with the papers for a few minutes, then Clint saw her move to near the door again. Tonio nodded the least bit and called, "Snra. Lange, come in here please."

She was right there, and he was looking directly at her. She came in. "Si?"

"Please call 'Nando Larencia, at the juego, and ask for an appointment, then get the files I will list ready."

"Si." She went out. Clint grinned at Tonio.

"Judge Larencia?"

"His name comes up too often in this. I'm going

to innocently ask him if he can remember a few little details that seem to be lost here. I found a couple of things that aren't in the records she'll bring. I'll see how he reacts to what I ask, and if he gives me the real information."

"If not, he's a biggie in it? How will he handle it? Got a guess?"

Lange came to the door to say, "The judge has a full calendar today. He can see you at ten thirty in the morning, if that is suitable?"

"It's not, but it's what we have. Very well."

She went back to her desk, which was not the one she went to when Clint looked like he was heading for the door.

"So. Now she can fix the files, maybe? They're ones I looked at last evening. I have copies of the pertinent parts."

Clint grinned. "I think maybe we can light a fire or two under that one."

"Let's not get into tired cliches. I'm tired.

"I seem to have asked Lange for files that aren't about what I wanted to cover with him. It will seem that a couple of other things came up between now and tomorrow morning."

"We can spend some time comparing the things you've learned with what I've learned," Clint suggested.

"After lunch. I didn't have anything except this

horrible office coffee this morning."

They went to a little restaurant for local food. It was delicious.

They met and compared notes. Clint would go with Tonio to the judge in the morning. He went back to the internet for the rest of the day.

In the morning he and Tonio made one more comparison. It was easy to see what had been excised from the police records. Clint noted one more time that, once something was on the net, it could never be completely erased again.

As they were going up the steps at the Ciudad Judicial Tonio got a call. It seemed that the thug involved with the sheik thing was killed last week in his cell. Apparently a fight with other inmates.

"Use the grapevine to let it be known that whoever did it will be next. He has to be stupid not to know that he's now the link to whoever's behind it. They have to silence him, then the one who silences him will be silenced."

Tonio nodded. "I thought of that. Maybe we'll get someone who wants to save his own worthless ass!"

They went in and to the judge's reception room, where they waited half an hour. They took it as a matter of course. This was a standard ploy.

Judge Larencia was a slightly pudgy, nervous,

small man with an air of being busy, so hurry it up!

"I just have to get a little information about a case you were involved with about a year and a half ago. That Mediterranean Sheik thing where he was a phony king or something. It seems one of the people convicted was released and is now dead, murdered (the judge looked shocked, and a little scared), along with Superior Judge Sardina. Considering that Sardina was the one who found the technicality that resulted in Itumi being out of prison, the connection is obvious."

"Er, Sardina? Wasn't he hit by a car or something? I don't know about any Itumi."

"He was killed, along with Itumi, and then run over by a truck," Clint said. "Modern methods make that kind of thing very easy to uncover."

"Er, uh."

"What we need is to know a few things about the days after the trial. The records show that you reviewed it and found nothing wrong, at the time. To know what needs investigation, we must know exactly how blatant the purported technicality Sardina found appeared to you, for one thing."

"Well, er. I didn't think it was very serious, if the truth be told, but it was Judge Sardina's case, and he was questioning his own process."

"But you did note that the bag was reported

opened at the trial?"

"Er, no. I would have called attention to that, but it was handled in sidebar, so didn't appear in the open records, you see."

"Then Sardina was remiss in not delaying the trial until conformation when it was first reported to him?" Clint asked.

"Well, er. Not remiss, exactly. Perhaps not too, er, careful, can we say. It should have been noted in open court records to avoid any possible future ramifications, if you will."

"Yes. There were definite ramifications," Tonio said. "You can see why we're concerned. Corrupt or not, a judge was murdered. We have to prevent that kind of thing, or judges will become afraid to make the proper rulings against those ladrones. Anyone else who was involved in that corruption is at risk, now. The hired thug they used was murdered in his cell. There's no way anyone can protect their ass from those people."

Every time Tonio mentioned "Murder" or "Murdered" Larencia flinched.

"I didn't know about that!" Larencia squealed. "Murdered? In his cell? In jail?" He was sweating, and visibly shaking. His voice was up, and he was whining. Clint raised an eyebrow at Tonio, who shrugged. Clint smirked and put a palm down below the desk, where Larencia couldn't see it.

"We know about this kind of thing. It may be connected to some of ... what you call mafia, here .. people. It puts anyone who dealt with them in any way at risk. It's how they operate. You'd think a judge would know better than to get himself into a situation that's exactly like he's had to try, but it seems everyone thinks they're exempt, for some reason. Nobody is!"

"I see. I'll have to spend some time with this. If you will give my secretary a list of the questions you will need answered I'll get to it as soon as possible. I have another appointment, now, I'm afraid."

He looked like he would die of heart failure at any second. Clint and Tonio stood, thanked him for his time as though nothing was wrong, and left. Tonio told the secretary he would send over a list of questions he needed answered. She said she would see to it.

Clint pointed to the intercom box when she turned toward a woman sitting in a chair and said to go on in. It had the little red light lit. She was listening to every word in there.

As they went down the steps, Clint said, "We don't have to find the thug's killer. Larencia is going to spill every little thing he knew. I think he actually shit in his pants when you said the thug was murdered in his cell."

Tonio nodded and looked grim. "Yes, and you said a couple of things we have to heed about their methods in there."

Too true!

Clint cleaned up and dressed for a night in the town. David is a tranquil, laid-back city that is more like a big village. The people are, mostly, very friendly.

It had been a few weeks since Clint was in David. He went to Las Brasas for a great rib-eye steak dinner, then went back into town. He talked with a young couple from Germany at the Parque Cervantes about the best places to see on a short vacation, then went to the Park Vista (Peter's) bar for a Balboa. He talked with several people, then went to another popular place. Gordo was no longer at Sandy's, and the music had changed. Gringos didn't go there much anymore, but there was a bar called Sasa across from the Pinzon Market that was becoming very popular. He went there and met Luz and Albert, the two who ran the place. Luz spoke English well, and was a very pretty and intelligent girl who had the perfect personality for the place. He stayed longer than he usually stayed in a place. Dave and Alan came in, then Aaron. The place was busy, but Luz still made time to talk with everyone for a bit. This was definitely a place he would come when he was in David!

It was about ten fifteen when he left to go to the Parque Cantina for a quick beer. Several of the regulars greeted him and chatted. Steve was there, and reminded Clint that they had met at the Conde a couple of months ago. Clint remembered, and asked about a couple of the people there.

Several people came to the door at times to look over the crowd, then left. Clint noted them all, subconsciously, a habit he'd worked long and hard to develop, like his great peripheral vision. He particularly noted one he'd seen hanging around the judicial. He seemed out of place here.

Roberto, a local vendor who came in when he closed his street corner salchica stand, came over to joke and talk. It seemed that a sour old tourist woman had seen Clint talking to a very pretty young blond girl in the park and was scandalized that a forty five year old man was hitting on a girl who couldn't have been more than seventeen or eighteen.

"I told her the girls here liked the older men, and nobody considered it any business of others. When she described you, I said that you were a very famous detective, and that you weren't forty five, you were in your fifties, and you didn't hit on young girls, they hit on you.

"I think it was that pretty German girl your were talking to."

"She's nineteen and with her boyfriend. I wasn't hitting on anyone. I'm sixty one.

"I agree. If I was hitting on her it wasn't anyone else's business except her boyfriend, who should knock me on my ass if I hit on his girl.

"Oh, hell! Was the woman that fat gringa with brassy red dyed hair? About fifty, herself?"

"Uh-huh. She wanted to hit on you and you were talking with a pretty young girl. She got jealous."

"She was almost comical trying to catch my eye. She wouldn't have any trouble getting dates if she'd lose thirty pounds and let her hair go natural."

"She could go down near the terminal. The guys there like big women."

They joked about the pathetic way some tourists acted, then Clint said he'd have to get some sleep, so he'd better call it a night. He waved at everyone and went out and headed along past the taxi stand and to the Costa Rica. He noted a car that was parked in front of the farmacia that started and pulled out as he went through the taxi stand, so was ready when it came along the street behind him. It pulled alongside and suddenly accelerated as a shot was fired that went right through the spot his head had occupied a half second earlier. His peripheral vision caught the hand with a pistol in it just inside the window, and he suddenly dropped. The car sped away. A black 2010 Honda four door – with a small oval dent just under the passenger side read door handle and a red and white *se vende* sign in the back.

That sign would be gone, now. It was there for anyone who might see it to use in identification.

The shooter would believe he had hit Clint, so he laid on the path (it was so broken up it could hardly be called a sidewalk anymore) until the car was slewing around the corner in front of Toro, then got up as a man and woman ran from the taxi stand to him.

"Dios mio! They tried to kill you!" the man cried.

"It's not the first time that's happened," Clint replied, with a tight smirk. "Thank you for your concern, but I'm alright. It's because I'm working with the police here to stop a corrupt bunch at the Ciudad Judicial."

"Ha! You are definitely *not* going to make any headway there!" the woman replied. They all laughed and Clint went on to the Costa Rica and sacked out.

He'd have to remember to tell Tonio about the assassination attempt in the morning. He wasn't the shoot-em-up type, but he was the one who said this bunch used exactly those methods.

In the morning Clint strolled around town while it was quiet. He was down by the Alcalá hotel, so went around to Doña Amelia's restaurant for a breakfast of hojaldras, bolitas, and coffee, then walked back toward the park and through. He wanted to be noted.

"Excuse me!" a voice called. The red-headed woman from yesterday was waving at him. He groaned inwardly and said, "Yes?"

"I'm new here. I just got here yesterday late, and don't know anyplace to find anything here. Could you recommend a good restaurant?

"Not those things like that Multi-Café place that's just like any restaurant anywhere. Something with local flavor, if you know what I mean. I don't have anyone to show me the places." She was batting her eyes and posing enough to almost make him laugh out loud.

"They have a lot of the local things there, but I just walk away from downtown when I want the local foods. I like them better than the standard gringo fare.

"Just go three or four blocks in almost any direction and walk along the street. There are small restaurants everywhere. Some are pretty good, others average."

"Well, I'm a single woman in a strange place, and I was told it can be dangerous. Would you like to have breakfast somewhere? My treat!"

"You're perfectly safe, here in David. The men will whistle and hit on you, but it's more a macho thing where they feel obligated to do that than serious."

"Oh, go on! Nobody is going to hit on some, fat, ugly, old gringo!"

"You have a lot to learn about Latin America! You're a long way from ugly, and a lot of the men here like big women. I think I saw you here last night. Surely you noticed that at least half the hookers are larger women."

"I ... hookers? What does that have to do with how...?"

"The hooker has to deliver what the men want, or she's out of business. Add it up!"

She suddenly had a bright gleam in her eyes, and an almost excited look. Clint continued, "Down near the terminal the girls we're taught are real sexpots in the states don't have a chance. The men think they're too skinny and ugly. The heavier women are the beauty standard among most of them."

"But ... I mean ... I don't want to look like a hooker! I can't tell if they are or not!"

"If you wear fancy shoes and walk with your chest thrown out and look men in the eyes with your head slightly lowered, like this (he lowered his head and turned slightly toward the side and looked in her eyes with a very small smile), you're probably hooking. They also wear those bras that push your breasts in and up."

"I will surely know what to avoid!"

"You never know. It might be fun to attract attention that way, but play it way down if you go near the terminal. They might not want to take no for an answer."

"For a woman who is fat and past it, you don't know what kind of fantasy we can make up if what you're saying is true!"

"It's a lark. Have fun! I have an appointment with a judge, so have to take a rain check on that breakfast. Have a great day!"

She nodded, and he walked away. He wouldn't be in the least surprised if he saw her near the terminal tonight – wearing fancy shoes, a squeeze bra, and cutting her eyes sideways at every man who walked past.

He went on toward the taxi stand. He would go to the station and meet with Tonio to make plans about what to do about the assassination attempt.

He got out and went to the gate. There was a black 2010 four door Honda with an oval dent

just under the passenger side rear door handle
parked two cars down from the gate.
  Veddy inderesdink!

Clint went into the station and to Tonio's office. Tonio waved him to a chair. He was on the phone. After about two minutes he hung up and said, "So? You managed to get shot at?"

"You heard about that?"

"Some woman saw it. She said you told her you were trying to break up the corrupted bunch at judicial, and that you laughed about being shot at. You told her you expected it, and it wasn't the first time."

Clint laughed. "Well, we *have* to break that shit up now, or I'll be the laughing stock of David!"

They spent awhile longer planning how to make Larencia break down. It was going to be almost automatic. He was terrified, and their point about nobody who could testify about anything getting knocked over had hit home. After about an hour, Clint said he had some internet work to do. When would they see the judge?

"Tomorrow at ten."

Clint went to the internet company to look up the ownership of a black 2010 Honda. He had the license plate number. It would be easy enough.

He wasn't sure he should let Tonio know about it. He saw too many coincidences here. He might be totally innocent, as Clint believed, but it could put him in the spot where he'd become the next assassination attempt.

The Honda was registered to Ana Castillo Perez Santos. She was a police officer on patrol duty.

It was no woman who shot at him.

Was it?

He didn't know. It could have been, but that would take away the one who Clint noticed at the Parque Cantina.

Why was the car parked right outside of the police compound? Wasn't anything ever going to make sense in this mess?

He called the police compound and asked to speak with Ana Castillo. He was told she wasn't there. She wasn't on duty until five o'clock. Five PM until two AM. She would be on patrol and couldn't answer the phone. Leave a number and she would be given a message. She could call him if she so desired.

Very interesting. She was on patrol last night when her car was used in an attempt to kill him. She wasn't driving it.

Who was?

Clint went back to the station and asked Tonio to get in touch with her. It was important.

Tonio called and got her sister, who woke her up. She said her car was at the compound last night, as far as she knew.

"You know it's parked on the street right out front of the compound right now?" Clint asked.

"No. It's right here."

"You're sure?"

There was a pause. "Yes. Right here. I can see it outside the window."

"It's a black 2010 Honda?"

"No. It's a blue Mitsubishi. Why?"

"Check the license plate!"

There was a three minute wait, then, "It's not there. What's going on?"

"It seems that your license plate was used in a murder attempt. Last night, about ten to twelve."

Clint thanked her and said to file that the plate was stolen. He would leave a declaration about the attempt and the fact the plate was outside the compound on a black Honda.

He thought for a few seconds, then went out. The car was gone. He went to the gate to ask the gateman if he'd noticed the car.

"There was a man who came just five minutes ago and drove away."

"Where did he come from?"

"I think he had crossed the street at the corner, coming from up toward the left."

"Did he do anything other than get in the car and leave?"

"I believe he took out something in the trunk and threw the wrapping in the trash can there, then he got in and drove away."

Clint went to look in the indicated trash can. There was a manila envelope that was addressed to C. Faraday. It had the license plate and a note inside.

Bad news, Mr. Faraday. Bad things can happen to good people. Perhaps Bocas would be a better place for you.

"Bad news, alright. But bad things can happen to bad people, too!" Clint said quietly.

He went back inside and dropped the envelope on Tonio's desk. Tonio raised an eyebrow and opened it.

"Did you touch anything?" he asked, slipping on latex gloves.

"Only using these," Clint replied, showing him his own pair of latex gloves. He always carried them.

Tonio took a CSI fingerprint kit from a drawer and dusted the envelop, note and plate. He didn't expect anything from the envelope, but found four sets. His and Clints were the easiest to identify. The others would be investigated.

The note didn't have anything. The plate had

two sets, one of which was Ana's and the other unknown, but not one that was on the envelope.

"We can try to find someone with a match," Tonio said. "We have three to investigate. Maybe we'll find someone with some connection.

"Any connection will have to help. We don't have anything unless we can get it from Larencia.

"We can go on to judicial. I won't be surprised if the honorable judge is on sick leave or something."

"You have his home address?"

"Yes, of course. We have to be able to respond quickly in case of immediate threat or whatever."

"We can go calling directly if he's not at the office."

"We're restricted *very* strongly about going to a judge's home."

"But you also are to respond quickly if there's a direct and immediate threat. There is."

Tonio nodded and stood. "We may as well go to judicial and get this part over with."

They took a police car and were at the court building at a quarter to ten. Larencia hadn't called in sick or anything else. He wasn't there.

"Call his home! Now!" Tonio ordered. "He's in danger! Tell him not to allow anyone inside his property except the police, and then only if I'm with them!"

She looked terrified. She grabbed the phone to punch autodial for Larencia. Clint asked why they couldn't get the closest officer to be there waiting for them.

"The license plate was stolen from the police compound. Only an officer with identification could get in there."

"I see. We might just get the wrong one to respond."

They raced out as soon as the secretary reported there was no answer, and the line wasn't busy. She called Larencia's private cellular number. It was turned off.

"This begins to look bad! Very, very bad!" Tonio said as they got in the car.

"How deep is this corruption in the courts and police here?" Clint asked.

"From the local street sweeper to the judges. I wonder mightily how much higher it goes. It is from a higher position than a judge, already."

"They don't care how much they hurt Panamá? They don't care about killing investment?"

"They're politicians. They care, first through tenth point, about their own pockets. That's what politicians are here."

"That's what they are everywhere."

They reached Larencia's house in San Antonio. It was a big mansion that had all kinds of security. The main gate was open, so they drove in and to the house. There was no answer to the door.

"I don't like this!" Tonio moaned. They went around the house, but there was no unlocked door and no open window. There was no sign of any forced entry.

"So! He let someone in he knew," Clint suggested. "Surely he wouldn't let anyone in who was involved in the payoff end!"

"Or perhaps a police officer with a story. He has a wife and two children. I'm very much afraid of what we may find when we go in."

Clint thought for a few seconds, then said he could go one more time around to see if there was a way in. Tonio could go to the car and call for backup and whatever they needed in the way of a warrant. Tonio started to say something, then nodded and went around front. Clint took a thin steel card he carried out and tried the door where he was. It had a deadlock that wouldn't move. He tried another, then the laundry room door, which opened easily. The door from there to the house was a little more difficult, but it did open.

Tonio came in behind him, said he'd called for a warrant, but had said an aide had found an open door, so send backup. He'd call if they needed the CSI or anything.

"You told them I found an open door."

"Yes. You're a rather resourceful person. I had no doubt you would discover a door that wasn't properly locked, or perhaps one that suffered a damaged mechanism."

Clint gave him the finger. They went in through the kitchen, expecting the worst. There was nothing out of place. There was no sign of anything being wrong.

"I would say our chicken has escaped the coop," Tonio said. "He has done what we should have recommended, but not the part where he goes with them."

"Yeah. Get your family to safety any way you can. He didn't seem the family type, so I didn't even consider it."

"We have to find what he left for us. He was ... my only contact with him before left me thinking he wasn't into anything this serious. He was too scared all the time. He would know he could never get out, once he was in.

"Clint, I will give him the benefit of the doubt.

It was all too possible his family was threatened as a way to make him comply with a crooked scheme. It is another way those people work."

"We have to find him, and we have to secure his family somehow. I think he knows he doesn't have a chance of staying alive a day if they find him."

"You think he left us something?"

"Consider: he knew we would be back today, and he knew we would demand some answers. He knew he would be erased as a problem before he could tell us anything. He knew we would come here first thing when we couldn't reach him, and he knew we would be in this house to find he was gone with his family. He knows he's dead, no matter what.

"He decided to protect his family. He couldn't, but we can.

"I think he knows the only way to protect them is if he's dead and they don't know anything. I think he wants revenge for what they plan."

"So they have no reason to attack his family if we have the information and they know nothing about it. He therefore protects his family and has his revenge."

"We can but hope that's the way it's going down." Clint looked thoughtful for a minute. "There's one other scenario here."

Tonio studied him. "What?"

"He seemed scared, but he seemed intelligent," Clint replied slowly. "Whatever he has, he also has some way to protect until he dies. I think he would bow to them to protect his family, but he will also have a very strong insurance policy, where they're concerned. He won't leave himself with no way out."

"Ah! So it will be in the court records in his own office safe! He must issue permission for anyone to see those files, and that is until his death or being removed for cause!"

"Exactly! He must issue permission. That's what's somewhere in this house."

The police detail came to the front door and called. Tonio went out to instruct them to place a policeman out of sight in three locations. They were to note and report, immediately, anyone who came there for any reason. The rest could return to the station. The emergency here was past.

He and Clint started searching the house. Clint stopped Tonio as they were going to start in the den/office. "It won't be in there. That's the first place anyone would look."

Tonio thought, then nodded.

Clint looked into each room. They were starting to go into the children's room when Clint shook his head. "That could put the children at risk."

Tonio agreed.

"It's either in the garage or in the laundry room. Barely possibly, the kitchen." Tonio nodded.

They went through the spotless garage. Unless it was very well hidden, it wasn't there. They were in the kitchen, but there didn't seem to be any-where anything could be hidden. They looked in all the drawers, as well as under them and behind them. There was just cutlery and towels and such. The refrigerator and washer guarantee papers, some electrical cords with special sockets for the coffee machine, and so forth, some small tools.

"Okay. The laundry room," Tonio said.

The laundry room was as spotless, but there were places to hide things there.

"I suppose we're probably looking for a manila envelope?" Tonio asked.

Clint started to nod, then shook his head. "I don't know. It could be."

Clint found it because the place was so totally spotless. There was a small smudge of grease on the bottom of the washer that was no larger than a quarter.

"That simply would not be here, but is some-thing a hood would miss," Clint said.

They searched the washer, finding nothing. Clint said it would be under the washer.

"I think it will be in the kitchen. I think I know

where it will be," Tonio suggested. "He wouldn't leave that smudge there if he had left it in that machine."

"I thought there couldn't be any other reason for it to be there. The washing machine was as much as tagged for us!"

"What did we see in the kitchen that has to do with the washing machine? That's already got some papers in it?"

"I'll be damned! Of course!" Clint cried. "The guarantee package! So! It'll be in the refrigerator envelope!"

"We think alike. We also think very much like Larencia does."

"*If* it's there."

"There is that."

It was. A little slip of an official form giving the holder, if he was a higher officer of the police or courts, special permission to search the appeals file cabinet in his private chambers. There was a slight smudge of the ink on the "V" in privado.

"We shall find something of great importance in the "V" file in the appeals cabinet," Tonio said.

"Shall we go?" Clint asked.

They got in the car and headed for the judicial.

"This should put the vice around a bunch of major corrupt slimewads!" Clint remarked.

"Don't make me laugh!"

They had to get Larencia's flowery signature authenticated before they could get access to the file. Larencia had included a fingerprint over the signature, so that was done quickly. The secretary said there must be an official observer. Tonio had Clint produce the papers stating he was a special consultant for the Policiá Nacionál, so that was done, as well.

They were shown into the chambers, where the secretary, M. Ariez, asked to be able to remain.

"You may, but consider that a judge and some thugs are already murdered because they knew what we're looking for. Larencia's now in hiding because he and his family are at risk. Do you really think it would be a good idea for you to also have that information?"

Her eyes were wide. Clint remembered the red intercom box light was on when they were in the chambers before.

"She already has a good part of it. This makes her know she'd be smart to get away from here to protect her ass!"

Tonio looked surprised and raised an eyebrow.

"When we were here before? The intercom?"

Tonio nodded. "Miss Ariez, it might be your only protection to tell us who and how."

"Dios mio! I ... I have a child! They will take my little girl!"

"Where is she, right now?" Clint demanded. "We can protect her and you."

"At the escuela. The Escuela Santa Maria por Niñas!"

"Who can you trust?" Clint asked Tonio, who shrugged.

"Call Ana, that officer from the license plate! Tell her to take that child to her place and secure it!"

Tonio took out his cell phone and called the station to ask for Ana's number again. He then called her and got her out of bed. She lived less than a kilometer from the school. She would have the maestro call for their confirmation when she was there. Seven minutes.

"Let's get the kid to safety before we look in that cabinet. We can talk with Mrs. Ariez," Tonio suggested.

Clint looked thoughtful, and shook his head. He pointed to the door and to Ariez. He told Tonio to stay with a finger down.

Ariez went with him to outside the door into the corridor. "Is that office bugged?"

"Bugs? I don't...?"

"Is there a surveillance or listening device in the chambers?"

"No. In the reception, maybe, but not in the judge's rooms. No one can get in there unless I know."

"Give me a name and let's get back as fast as we can."

"Name? I ... oh! I only know Javier D'Angelo. He's from Italy, and works for someone. I don't know who."

Clint nodded and pointed back inside.

"Coffee machine's not working," he said when he walked back inside the door, just inside the reception office. Tonio nodded. and said, "Shit! Let's get this done."

Clint pointed to the desk and Ariez. She looked questioning, then brightened slightly to say, "I will remain here at my duty. You may call on the call box if you find my presence necessary. Do not disturb any of the judge's files without proper cause."

"Very well. Promised," Tonio replied. They went into the chambers and closed the door. Clint said it wasn't likely there were any bugs in the private chambers, but there was at least one in the reception room. Ariez had seen to it that no one went inside the chambers when the judge wasn't there.

"Okay. We called for Ana and the kid from in here, so maybe the child will be safe, already, but we'll wait. Name?" Tonio asked.

"Javier D'Angelo, Italian."

"Contact or boss?"

"Contact, so far as she knows."

Ana called and Clint used the intercom to ask that Ariez come in to show them which files were included in the warrant. She came in and talked to the superintendent at the school, who let Ana take the seven year old girl out. She instructed the superintendent to tell anyone who asked about the girl that she would *not* be molested during classes, except by the mother, and it was improper to ask about a little girl who was not family and goodbye!

Ariez went back to her desk, looking greatly relieved that the girl was being taken to safety. Tonio and Clint went to the appeals files to find there was a combination lock on it. Ariez hadn't mentioned having the combinations.

"Permisso number four ten seventeen," Tonio said.

They tried it. Nothing. "Seventeen ten four," Clint suggested. That worked.

There was a thick manila envelope in the back of the files that had "Seguros" on it. Seguros =

insurance.

They took the envelope to the desk and opened it. It had some photographs and lists, along with a sheet of paper with a code number and nothing else. The code number was on a torn factura that only had "...quiNet" on the corner and B/0.65 on the total line.

"It's the passcode for something. We have to find what," Clint said.

"There'll be something in this office to tell us that. This picture is Donaldo Rauz Vega with a very big ... party man."

"Party?"

"Political party. Rauz is a known mobster type with some highly questionable methods of doing business.

"Here's a picture of Quinten Martín Quinteros with Falcuesta, the party head. He's another. Two of the three biggest mobsters here with him. That says ... I'll be damned! Pancho Gorchev! He's the big Panamanian-Russian mobster in Panamá City!"

"And this Rauz character is here? And Martín?"

"You got it Charlie!"

"We have to decode this, and we have to find where we go on the net. This should make a few waves!" Clint exulted.

"You *do* rather like understatement, don't you?"

They went back out, after relocking the cabinet. Tonio had the envelope under his shirt. He told Ariez that they found a code that didn't seem to mean anything, but they'd have the police experts work on it. If Larencia called, have him contact Tonio on his private celular.

"You expect him to call?" Clint asked.

"Yes. He will want me to know he did nothing he wasn't forced to do, and he will take a chance to tell me what the code means."

They went to the station. Clint said it might be a good idea not to use the police computers for this one. Tonio agreed, so they went to La Tipica for lunch, seeing it was so close, and the food was good, then to the internet company. Tonio had a list of the sites on the register from Larencia's computer.

"Okay. Where do you think we'll find what we want? How?" Tonio asked.

"Simple. We'll go to each site and try the pass code. The one it works on is it."

That seemed logical. They went to four forums and Facebook and Twitter and several others.

Nothing.

"It surely wouldn't be on any of his six e-mail sites?" Tonio asked.

"Which is exactly why we should have tried those first!"

It was on z-mail.com. They accessed the site and found very little. It was used to communicate with people who traveled in the Caribbean. He had met most of them on cruises with his family. He contacted them, they answered. Only two were a continuing exchange. There was nothing obvious there.

"This has to be it, but where?" Tonio asked.

Clint went to the z-mail home page and read everything there. There was a list of received mail and sent mail, an address book, and a draft listing. There were two messages in the draft section. To another of his e-mail carriers.

"Want to bet? They were never sent," Clint suggested.

"So? Go!"

Draft one said there were questions to be asked and answered about the route the Rauz boat was planning across the Caribbean to Cuba, then to Florida, then to Colombia. It may be difficult to go directly from Cuba to Florida.

"Okay. I think Rauz has connections in Cuba, Colombia, and Florida. I'd say drugs," Tonio said.

"Agree?"

"I'd give it fifty-fifty or less. I doubt it would be anything obvious. Itumi and group weren't into drugs *because* it was too easy to be caught, then nothing would work in the future. They were into money, mostly. I'd say counterfeit."

"Good chance!"

The next draft was about Brazil and the strong economy there.

"He's being too obscure with his clues! What could it be – unless the two drafts aren't related. Aren't *both* related. I'd say we concentrate on the Rauz boat route," Tonio suggested.

"Don't be too sure. What's the exchange rate?"

"But compared to Brazil or Cuba or Colombia? Exchange from which to which?"

"Panamá is the dollar, US. You know something? Brazil and Panamá share the top economies in Latin America. I think maybe we're dealing with counterfeit, but Reais!"

There was a long pause. "So! Smuggle them into Colombia, distribute them through Cuba and Colombia. Could be, and much harder to detect."

"And based on something more than a printing press."

"You lost me?"

"US money isn't based on anything anymore. Brazilian money is."

Tonio nodded. "Well, maybe we have ... a little bit of nothing! I still don't get it! This is hardly enough motive for anyone here to get killed. It's something between the US and Brazil."

"Unless the queer money is being exchanged for dollars here? Remember; Panamá uses the dollar. You can exchange for dollars at any bank that exchanges money. Get dollars and take them to the states. Rauz probably doesn't even have a boat that ever leaves Panamanian waters.

"I think maybe we should warn Cuba that it may be receiving a hell of a lot of Brazilian money in a laundering and exchange scheme."

He nodded again. "All we need is motive, which this supplies. Now we have to be able to tie someone directly into it. They'll think they're safe, there."

"If that were true we wouldn't have a certain note in a certain envelope with a certain license plate."

"I suppose we wouldn't. What do they think we know that we *don't* know?"

"If we knew that, we'd know."

That finally got him the finger.

"I think I'll go back to the pensión and try to think this out," Clint said. "There's something I'm supposed to know. It will be from my first encounter with that phony sheik."

"There was counterfeit then?"

"Not to any extent we knew about. It's just that the sheik affair was our only connection with this mess. It's much too possible this isn't directly related to that. It may only be that Itumi was in both things. He only connects with ... I'll be damned! Jewels! Colombia isn't necessary to the counterfeit part of this, so why is Colombia even mentioned?"

"Jewels?"

"It's complicated. Why would they think I'd even connect that? We're still with them thinking I know something I don't."

"With this, we can possibly ... we can't do a damned thing! We have to be able to tie them into something. Maybe we can set up something that will catch them for the counterfeit part. That will be something positive, but you have to have something that's solid. We almost have enough to grab this Javier D'Angelo character, but almost doesn't cut it."

Clint nodded and sighed. They talked a bit more, deciding to try to find D'Angelo and work from that point to somewhere else. Clint thought of the Firm's song, *I had no direction, I didn't even want to know where I was going.*

Didn't fit. He definitely wanted to know where he was going.

He went to the Costa Rica and spent the later afternoon, sitting at the front, chatting with the tourists and the regulars. He didn't learn anything new there, so cleaned up and headed for the new Mexican/ Honduran restaurant for his dinner.

There was a black 2010 Honda four door with a small oval dent just below the passenger side rear door handle sitting in front of the panaderia across the street. He noted the new license plate number and walked on out and around the corner to the right instead of to the restaurant. When he was out of sight near the Bocachica Restaurant he call Tonio, who was home by then. He gave him the license plate number. Maybe they had a minor break in this confused mess!

If it was for that car.

He had just rung off of the short message when the car came around the corner. He went on to the corner and turned toward Centro. The car could turn that way, so he went about twenty meters that way, stopped, snapped his fingers, and went back the way he'd come. The car had turned the corner and couldn't go back. It was one way.

Clint grinned to himself and went on around to the Mexican/ Honduranian Restaurant for a delicious meal. He then went to the Sasa bar, then back to the Parque Cantina. The black Honda was parked where it had been when they tried to assassinate him. He grinned and went inside.

The hood from before was sitting at the bar. He sat beside him and said, "Do they call you Javier or D'Angelo?"

"Beg pardon?"

"You're rather an amateur hit man. You can scare the locals, I guess. You can't scare me."

He grinned and laughed. "I'm not D'Angelo. He's in Panamá, at the moment.

"It wasn't me who shot at you. I only drive the car. I wouldn't miss, but I didn't think Wil ... he would either, at that distance. You looked like you were hit."

It fell into place for a tiny part. Will Cousins was a hit man with Itumi in the Bocas del Toro bit.

"I watched you. I had a little mirror focused on that window, so when the hand reached out, I dropped.

"Cousins hit the judge and Itumi? You?"

"Me, no. Cousins, I don't know. I don't think so. Not his MO. Maybe Lorenzo. He was here.

"I'm not after you, except to see where you go. You made me and threw me off, a bit earlier. When you stopped and snapped your fingers, I thought I'd like to blow your damned head off, then it was funny. You suckered me perfectly!

"I'm Jerry Berry, and no smart remarks. It's, unfortunately, my name."

"Well, if you're going to be following me you might as well let me ride with you. Save the taxi."

He laughed and toasted Clint with his beer. Clint ordered a Balboa and sat to chat with Berry and several people he knew. After a half hour he said he wanted to go to Brother's Bar to see if someone was there, then down near the terminal to see if someone else was there.

"Not to do with this money thing."

"Money thing?"

"Surely no one thought I couldn't connect the dots!"

He grinned and giggled. "I don't know about money, but I'm supposed to distract you to where you don't connect the dots."

"Didn't work. Itumi, the sheik ... how could I miss it?"

He shrugged. They went to Brother's Bar. Clint didn't really have a reason to want to go there, so he'd do things to make them wonder what he was up to. They had a beer, then went down near the terminal. Just as he thought. A red-headed heavy woman in a push-up bra and fancy red shoes was talking with three men at the chicken restaurant.

He hoped reality would come close to her fantasy.

"Might as well go back to Centro. Nobody here."

His celular rang. He answered. It was Tonio. "Rental car. Rented to a gringo who looks like a Panamanian. Jerald Berry."

"Thanks. We're talking right now."

"Learn anything?"

"Oh, yeah!"

"In danger?"

"Don't really know. I doubt he does, either. I'll let you know if anything comes up." He rang off and shook his head. "All I ever need is to *get* an answer before I can *give* one! Some people!"

"Woman trouble?"

"Aren't they all?"

He laughed. "I think I like you! You've got a sense of humor, even when I drove for a guy who tried to kill you."

"He missed. What he has to understand is that he's given me the right to blow his stupid fucking head off next time I see him. I should'a last time, in Bocas."

"In other words, he'd be smart to never cross your path again."

"Something like that."

"I was told you don't make noise, you just handle things your own way. Very professional."

"I prefer a quiet, easy lifestyle. I don't intrude on those people, they intrude on me. I tend to resent it."

He laughed. "We'd make good buddies, I think.

"I've heard a lot about a place called Esmeralda. Know it?"

"Yeah. It's Javier's place. Everyone in David knows about it. Colombian girls."

"Want to go?"

"No. I don't care for the atmosphere in those places. I'm weird, that way. Most of the people I know go there on a more or less regular basis. I'm married, and don't go after anyone else."

"Oh. Okay."

"Go if you like. I'm going to sack out, so you'd just get bored, sitting over there in the panaderia parking lot."

"I'd probably move over by the university so you wouldn't put it together that I was always right across the street. Thanks."

"I know two other easy ways to leave the Costa Rica that you couldn't watch from either place –

which I ain't telling you about."

"Yeah. I was warned that you have some great disguises, too!"

"Po l'll ol' *me?!*"

He laughed. He dropped Clint off in front of the pensión and drove off toward the Esmeralda. Clint believed he was actually going there like he believed rocks could swim.

Might as well really sack out. Let Jerry Berry be bored sitting where he could see the entrance.

So he did.

In the morning he worked about three hours on the computer, then took one of the secret ways out of the place and strolled around the corner and into the front. He waved at Berry, sitting in front of the Mexican restaurant, said, "What the hell?" and went there for breakfast. Berry came in and sat with him.

"Did you leave last night or early this AM?"

"Early this AM. I just wanted to demonstrate that you're wasting your time if I want to go anywhere without being seen. I get up about four thirty, usually, but had a lot to do on the computer this morning, so just now came out. I didn't believe for a picosecond you were actually going to the Esmeralda."

"Wrong! I did go to the Esmeralda. I was there until about two thirty."

"Are you going to be following me all day today, too?"

He shrugged. "I'll call in at eight and find out. I'll report about riding you around last night, and that you know a hell of a lot more than anyone ever guessed. I'll tell them you think they're a bunch of amateur clowns."

"You will?"

"Well, you do."

"Uh-huh. Want to go to the police station?"

"Not inside. They have very effective ways to make you say things, I hear."

"I doubt there's anything you could say that would do more than confirm what we already know."

"I could tell them who I report to."

Clint decided to take a chance. Only one of them was in David. "Rauz? We already know."

He looked shocked. It was the first time Clint knew definitely that he'd gotten a reaction out of him.

"That one leaves me wondering. I didn't give you that information, you gave it to me. All I know is that at eight o'clock I report to a voice at a certain number. I'd heard rumors that he was the one, but I always thought he was too big to be handling the mundane details."

"He's not too big to get his ass in a crack. Got to

be practical about these things.”

“I really do think I like you, no shit! You don’t ever pull your punches, and you don’t beat around. I find that’s rare. What you see is what you get.”

“Yeah. We’re here. Come on in. I’ll introduce you to the cast of players on the good-guy end.”

“That will be a new experience.”

He parked where he’d parked with the license plate thing and they went into the station and to Tonio’s office. Tonio raised an eyebrow as they came strolling into the office, and Clint said, “Jerry, Tonio. Jerry’s the driver for attempted assassinations and such things.”

“But not the assassin?”

“No. That was Cousins, as we suspected.”

Tonio hadn’t heard a word about any Cousins, but knew to play along with Clint. “Oh, him. No wonder he missed. Silly damned amateurs! If he’d hit you at all it would be a bloody mess and you’d live to get even – with massive interest.

“A Manolo called. He couldn’t get through to your celular, for some reason.”

Clint took out his celular. It was discharged. He sighed and used the desk phone to call his friend, a secret agent for Interpol, among others. They exchanged greetings and Manolo asked if he could be overheard.

"Yeah, something like that, I suppose."

"You know that certain powerful people are asking a lot of questions about you?"

"Those big mafia types, I suppose. Scared of the Ruskies and the local jokes."

"What's it about?"

"Oh, it's *always* about the money! They never learn that some people aren't into that shit! Who gives a damn how much they spent in Bogota and Rio! The only ones they impress are people just like them. Big fucking deal! Why would anyone want to? Bunch of phony-asses!"

"Phony money?"

"Yeah. Like everyone and his dog hasn't been to Rio."

"From there? To where?"

"Well, coming from the states to here allows you to go to Havana without a lot of crap. Cuba's alright, but mostly the cigars."

"Okay. I read phony Raeis going to the states and Cuba, being sent by those half-assed mafia types. What's Colombia got to do with it?"

"I really couldn't answer that. I wish I could."

"Want it stopped? Is it much?"

"It sounds like a killer deal. I think I'd take a chance. Go for it!"

"Good as done! Caio!"

"Who's Manolo?" Berry asked. "I know. It's

none of my fucking business."

"Not at all! He's a master spy and an agent for Interpol and that kind of everyday crap." Tell them the truth, and the last thing they'd do is believe it. Berry laughed and said he'd asked for that one.

Tonio didn't quite know how to react to Clint bringing an admitted hood into the office to make jokes. When Berry wasn't looking he raised the eyebrow. Clint grinned.

"It's eight. You can step outside to call Rauz," he told Berry, who laughed, and started to step outside. He stopped and took a cheap celular out of a pocket and punched the autodial. After a few seconds he said, "Rauz? I just wanted to report that Faraday is totally onto you and to us and everything and thinks it's funny that you'd think he gave a shit. I'm in the police station, right now, talking with a police captain and Faraday. They knew it was Cousins, but don't know if he was the one to do them the favor ((he gave a thumbs up to Clint) of knocking over Sardina and Itumi. They've been using Geraldo to get false messages from the station to us. They think, and I'm beginning to agree, that we're a bunch of amateur clowns.

"What?"

"It was pretty obvious. You wouldn't want me

working for you if I didn't check on that kind of thing."

"What difference does that make? They're the ones who told me about it."

"What?"

"Okay." He offered the phone to Clint.

"Yeah?"

"Mr. Faraday? You know who I am? How?"

"Certainly I knew who you were. All this going on, and you're the one here?"

"Now I'm vastly confused, Mr. Faraday. You seem to be playing a game of some sort. I don't think you know anything, you've just tricked Jerry into giving you a lot of information. He doesn't have the information you're seeking, so don't be too hard on him. I tend to rather like a man with a sense of humor, and he has that."

"Well, I guess you're right. He doesn't have a clue as to Reais and that kind of thing. Jerry doesn't. We do."

There was a silence. "What's the deal?"

"I didn't just take anything out of a hat. As soon as you had Sardina and Itumi hit a certain person in Rio called me. There is a rather large group of people who want to cut in. He works for the U ... for a large government who are watching you. They won't finance much more of a loss. They have about all of it."

"Rio? The USA isn't deeply involved, so your information is incomplete."

"The UK, not US."

Another longer silence. "So. We are not a step behind, we are a kilometer behind. I learn some very useful things from you."

"Keep as much of it as you can out of Panamá and we'll be easier to work with. Our big bitch is you using that corrupt bunch of slime in judicial in your silly plots."

"I tend to agree that was a terrible mistake. I argued against it. There seem to be an inordinate number of such people there."

"Slime collects in puddles."

"I like that! I will try to make arrangements to move the main operation elsewhere."

"It won't do any good. They're about to take the problem out of the equation." Another pause. "I wish I knew how much they know."

"Almost everything. They don't need any absolute facts. They operate much the same as you. We have to have it all. Almost, as Tonio said, doesn't cut it with the law here."

"Thank you, Mr. Faraday. It would be wise for me to extract myself from this operation?"

"Very. And one other thing, please?"

"Yes?"

"Don't involve innocent people in your crooked

schemes. It will make me move against you"

"I don't...?"

"Judge Larencia was terrorized into helping you as a way to protect his family. He wasn't badly corrupt, but was forced into it. His family are innocent of anything. If anything unpleasant were to happen to any of them I would feel obligated to very personally come after all of you."

"I think I do not wish for that to ever happen. You may tell them that I will call you. That was not of my doing. I will guarantee their safety as soon as I can make a point or two to my, er, business associates in this venture.

"May I speak with Jerry, please?"

Clint handed the phone to Berry, who listened a minute, then replied, "I tried to warn you that he always knew a hell of a lot more than we ever guessed. I think you can take his word, exactly as stated. He doesn't bother with subterfuge."

"You, too. I'll hang around here or go?"

"I'd rather hang around. Clint and I have an understanding. I can call him a buddy."

"No. Buddy. Friend will take awhile. He's not the type to rush into things." He listened a minute, then laughed and rang off.

"Clint, we are not to get intimate, as it has been suggested you do with your Indio friends, until I know you won't use it against me."

"Damn! And I was wondering if you'd be a good fuck!" That got him the finger from both Tonio and Berry.

Berry said, if it was okay with them, he hadn't gotten much sleep in three days, so would like a chance to sack out for a few hours. Tonio said they didn't have a lot to do, so why not?

Berry left. Clint said it would be a good time to get a bite. He might go back to Bocas tomorrow.

"Oh! I wish Jerry hadn't told Rauz we know about Geraldo. He's redundant, from this point," Clint said.

"Oh, yeah. I guess we don't have much reason to try to make them think we fell off the turnip truck this morning anymore." He raised an eyebrow at Clint. Clint wrote a quick note: *Do you know which Geraldo?* Tonio nodded. *Get him here.*

Tonio used the intercom to tell the desk to send Geraldo Garcia in. They waited a few minutes, and he came in, looking like a whipped dog.

"You don't have to say it. I know I'm fired, but will you charge me?"

"No," Clint answered. "Just take your little bugs with you. We can't use them anymore, either."

"Thanks." He went to take a small knick-knack off the bookshelf and a pen from the desk holder. He then walked out.

Tonio shook his head and they went out.

"This just in.

"Shortly after midnight last evening a special team of officers from Panamá, the EE. UU., and the United Kingdom stormed three locations in Panamá, one here in David, one in Santiago and one in Panamá City. A reported three hundred million ... wow! ... false Reais, Brasilian money, were seized. The operation was arranged through Interpol, and there were like seizures in Cuba, England, Israel, and Florida, EE. UU.

"Officers in charge, Major Bottoms of the EE. UU. and Admiral Le Bonne of Francia, state that a secret Interpol agent stationed here in Panamá was responsible for the information leading to the operation that could badly affect the basic economies of many countries.

"We are not as of yet apprised of the complete results of the stormings in those other countries, and only partly about the operation in Panamá. We are to understand that several persons fired upon the officers, and were in turn fired upon. A Mr. Cousins and a Mr. Levens, foreigners, and Pablo Encanto Perez, Panamanian, were killed in the action.

"More as it is reported.

"In other news, the problem of the hydroelectric project in...."

Clint sighed and tuned the rest out. They had, as usual, left out some parts of the story that had to be exposed if there was to be progress against the ingrained corruption in the court system.

He went in the kitchen to pour himself another cup of coffee. He heard, "News flash! This now arriving!

"Judge Larencia, of the Superior Court, has just this hour issued subpoenas against nine people he said had tried to coerce him into corrupt acts in the money counterfeiting scheme reported on this station earlier. He declares, in sworn deposition, that these people threatened him and his family. He worked with the police and with well-known private police consultant Clinton Faraday to bring these acts into the spotlight of the courts.

"'My part was simply to play the victim and to attempt to have those persons make statements that were recorded and filmed that would prove our case. I have submitted some of those photographs that show meetings between officials to be named when the subpoenas are served and known crime syndicate heads. I will keep the public informed as to our progress. As many are aware, it is most difficult to prosecute these people, because witnesses will find themselves in the position of defendant, not accuser. That is a part which must be changed in the law.'

"Judge Larencia claims he had to take his family, a wife and two small children, into hiding in Costa Rica to insure their safety from those people.

"This station will keep you informed of further events in this matter.

"Now to sports. Bocas del Toro has triumphed over Los Santos in the game last...."

Larencia wasn't deeply involved. Maybe this would be the platform he would use to run for president or something. He did make it look like he was in on the exposure of an international plot. Or maybe not. Clint doubted he'd vote for him.

C. D. Moulton's works are available on most major outlets as printed or e-books. CD writes the CD Grimes, PI mysteries, the Det. Lt. Nick Storie mysteries, the Clint Faraday mysteries, the Flight of the Maita science fiction series, books on orchid culture and many others of many types. Mystery, adventure, intrigue, science fiction, fantasy, paranormal, mild erotica, and factual.

www.ingramcontent.com/pod-product-compliance
Lightning Source LLC
Chambersburg PA
CBHW052227150726
48002CB00003B/1306